That Wonderful Summer

LUCILLE E. HEIN

Judson Press ® Valley Forge

*A thank-you to Canada where my sister and
I travel as often as we can—having many experiences,
meeting many people, and enjoying the great
natural beauty.*

THAT WONDERFUL SUMMER

Copyright©1978
Judson Press, Valley Forge, PA 19481

The name JUDSON PRESS is registered as a trademark in the U.S. Patent Office.
Printed in the U.S.A. ⊕

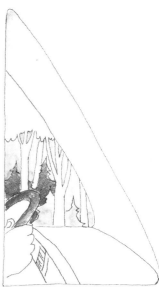

"Will we be there soon?" Mark asked.

"Soon," Mother said.

Mark, his mother and father, and a driver
were in the roomy cab of a tow truck,
lurching and bumping along a logging road
that went north into the wilderness.
A long trailer lurched behind the truck.

The trailer, which would be set up at the end of the
       road,
would be their home for the summer
while Mark's father worked in the wilderness for his
       company.

"Will we be there soon?" Mark asked again.

It seemed to Mark that they had been riding forever.
They had stored their car at the last camp;
the driver with his tow truck had picked them up
       there.

Since then, Mark had seen only forest
and the rutted road the driver followed.

"When we get there, what's there?" Mark asked.

"More forest, a huge lake," his father said.

"Can I swim there? Is there a boat?"

"We hope so."

"Why are the leaves so small?" Mark asked.

"It's still spring here, though it is June.
We had spring in April at home."

"Will there be anyone to be my friend?"

"Maybe not," Mark's father said.
"But you will find your own fun."

"Doesn't the ranger have a daughter?" Mother
        asked.

"Oh, yes, I had forgotten.
He told me that when we met this spring
at the international conservation meeting," Father
        answered.
"Will she like me? Will I like her?" Mark asked.

"We will like everyone," Mother assured Mark.
"There are few people. We will know them all.
No city crowds—what a wonderful summer!"

The forest grew deeper and darker.
Mark sat in the truck—quiet, lonely.

But he tried to be happy.
"Maybe it will be a wonderful summer," he said.

By late afternoon their trailer was set up
in a small clearing at the edge of the lake.

Mark ran a few feet to the beach. "Can I swim
            here?" he asked his father.

"Sure! I do!" a voice came from behind him.

Mark spun around and saw a girl his age.
He was suddenly shy.

"Hello!" Father spoke for Mark.
"Are you Gina, the ranger's daughter?
Are you alone?"

"Yes. Daddy says I'm old enough now—
and careful enough—to come here alone
if I take the easy path along the shore.
I have a note for you," she said.

Gina gave the note to Mother. Then she spoke to
        Mark.
"Hello! Will you stay all summer?
May I look in your trailer?
Do you like to cook and eat outdoors?"

Mother laughed. "Take Gina to the trailer.
Maybe she will help you unpack."

"Come on!" Mark shouted, no longer shy.
"Yes. I like to cook and eat outdoors."

"You're eating outdoors tonight—with us.
Mother's invitation is in that note."

"How will we go to your house?
There's no road. We left our car behind."

"Mother sent me to show you the trail."

Gina helped Mark open his boxes and bags.
She saw his field glasses. "May I use them?"

"Sure. Use them all you want."

Gina focused them. "Wish I had glasses."

"My grandparents gave them to me," Mark said.
"They thought I would be alone all summer.
They didn't know about you!"

"You let me share your glasses, Mark,
and I'll share my secret places with you—
in the forest, at the lake, around the bogs."

Mark was a bit scared by the wilderness.
It was so lonely, so empty, so wild, so vast.

But he saw that Gina was not scared.
He said to Father, "Gina is never afraid."

"That is because she has always lived here.
Her parents teach her about the outdoors.
They teach her to be careful, not afraid.
Gina might be afraid in the city."

"Pooh! Who's afraid of the city?" said Mark.

"You live in the city and like it.
Gina might not like the noise and crowds.
Let Gina teach you about the north woods.
Then you will not be afraid."

Later, when he was with Gina, Mark asked,
"Are there any bears here?"

"Some. They come when the berries are ripe."

"Are there any deer?"

"Lots. Haven't you seen any yet?"

"Are there any people here?"

"Until you came, no one lived near us."

"Are there any roads?"

"No. Your trailer is at the end of the road.
To go farther north, we backpack
or go by boat or by bush plane.
There are many trails for campers and hikers."

"Who made the trails?" Mark asked.

"Indians, explorers, hunters, hikers. . . ."

"Indians! Are there Indians here?"

"A few. Daddy often works with Indians."

"Do you know any Indians well? Really well?"

Gina nodded. "One—Tabera.
Tabera's cabin is on Lost Lake.
Daddy takes me if he is passing her cabin.
Then Tabera and I have a day together."

"Could I visit her?" Mark asked hopefully.

"Tabera wants me to bring you. Soon!"

"Br—r—r! Cold!" Mark shivered.

Gina laughed. "Only your toes are wet!
The water is always cold here.
You're used to a city pool with warm water."

Mark clenched his fists, jumped into the water,
    gasped.
But once he was wet, he was warm.

"We must stay where Mother can see us," Gina said.
"She's in the garden. She's our lifeguard."

Gina ducked under and brought up a small pebble.
"Look, Mark! It's shiny, like a jewel.
I collect pretty stones."

"What can I collect?" Mark asked.
"Stones are too heavy to take back to the city."

Gina looked about. "Collect feathers.
I often find feathers lost by birds.
Or I collect leaves and press them,
or collect flowers. But be careful
and take only one of each flower."

"Why?"

"You know why!
We must protect all things in nature—
all things that are God's.
That's what your father and my father do.
That's their job."

Mark stubbed his toe on something on the sandy
     bottom.
"Ouch!" He pulled up a piece of gray wood.

"I'll collect driftwood," he decided.
"Pieces that look like animals, birds, fish.
Pieces that are satiny and shiny.
Pieces that I can pack and take home."

"That piece is a driftwood bird," Gina said.

"Gina! Mark!" Gina's mother called.
It's time to come and play in the warm sand."

Mark showed Gina's mother the driftwood.
"I collect driftwood. What do you collect?"

"Bird songs. I whistle and sing bird songs."

"Will you whistle some for me?"

"Yes. Some day we will sit quietly, listen,
and then try to whistle and sing like birds."

Gina did not forget her promise
to show Mark her favorite, secret places.

One morning she came to his trailer early,
a plastic lunch bag tied to her belt.

"Daddy is hiking upstream to test water.
I hope Mark can go with Daddy and me,"
she said as she gave a note to Mark's mother.

"Of course Mark can go. What fun!"

"I'm taking you to my secret cave,"
Gina said to Mark as they hiked with her father.

The trail went around a marsh
where fat frogs plopped;

into the deep forest
where animal eyes watched them;

through a burned-over area
with stumps of trees, sad and black;

into a low brush area
where scratchy twigs caught their clothes;

to a stream bubbling over rocks,
whose song they heard as they neared it.

Gina took Mark's hand. "Come!" she said.
They forded the stream on flat stones.

"Here's my secret cave. Only Daddy knows it."
Gina pointed to a ledge in a rock cliff.
Rocks hung over the ledge like a roof.

"I sit here and pretend I am an explorer
taking shelter from a storm," Gina said.
"Or an Indian watching for a fox."

"How do you reach your cave?" Mark asked.

"Put your foot here. Grab this root."

Mark and Gina scrambled to the ledge.
Gina untied her lunch bag. "Shall we eat?
Daddy will be busy for a while.
We can do what we want
just so we stay near him.
We must never go alone into the forest."

"Look!" Mark whispered, trying not to squeal.

"A doe," Gina said. "And two fawns with her."

Mark passed his field glasses to Gina.
"Did you ever pet a deer?" he asked.
"I did—at a zoo."

"Deer are wild animals. You don't pet them.
You don't put them in cages," Gina explained.

Gina's father shouted from upstream,
"Gina! There's a new bridge here."

Gina and Mark raced along the bank.
A dead tree had fallen over the stream.
They crossed and recrossed the new bridge.

Mark thought the day was wonderful.
At bedtime he told Mother about his day,
about Gina's cave, the deer, the tree-trunk bridge.

"Why don't you tell God about it?" Mother said.
"God made the day for you."

"I will," Mark said.
        "Dear God, thank you for giving me today.
        It was fun. Amen."

"Tomorrow Gina's father and I go by boat
to visit a mining camp," Mark's father said.
"We will leave you and Gina with Tabera,
Gina's Indian friend."

The next morning the four started early in the
        motorboat.
They left the big lake
and went through a river and two small lakes
to Tabera's lake, a calm, round pond.

Gina waved. "Tabera's in her garden," she said.

Tabera greeted Gina and her father,
"Good to see you. And you bring friends?"

"This is Mark and his father," Gina said.
"Our fathers are going to the mining camp.
May we stay with you for the day?"

"Sure. You can help me gather rocks.
I'm building a new outdoor baking oven."

"An outdoor baking oven!" Mark shouted.

"You've never baked outdoors?" Tabera asked.

Mark liked Tabera.
She wore dark pants and a plaid shirt.
Her black hair swung in a long braid.
Her necklace was made of bright, polished pebbles.

Tabera's log cabin was one big room.
It contained a huge, stone fireplace for cooking and
      heating,
a cot bed, a table, and log seats.
On one wall were shelves holding driftwood.

"I collect driftwood," Mark said proudly.

"Tabera polishes and stains driftwood
and makes it into beautiful things," Gina said.
"She sells them at art shows, stores, and big resorts."

"Yes," Tabera said. "I make my living
from the dead wood that God sends to shore.
Which piece do you like, Mark?"

"This." Mark pointed to a small log slab.
A quivering wire rose from the slab.
On the wire soared a driftwood bird.

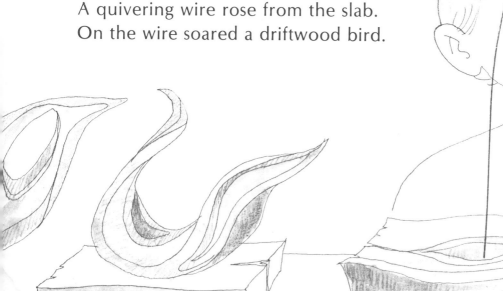

All day Mark did things he had never done before.
He and Gina followed Tabera like puppies.
They picked berries.
   They gathered garden vegetables for soup.
      They looked for rocks for the outdoor oven.
         They fried fish outdoors.
            They helped polish pebbles and drift-
            wood.

The smell of soup floated over the clearing.
Tabera added herbs to the pot. "We'll eat now," she
      said.

After lunch Mark and Gina wandered about
      Tabera's place.
They looked at everything—log cabin, garden, tiny
      spring,
sunny clearing, sparkling lake,
black forest surrounding everything.

When they heard the motorboat,
they ran to the shore and shouted and waved.

In the boat Mark was tired and so happy.
He leaned against Father, waved to Tabera.

"Come again!" Tabera called. "Come soon!"

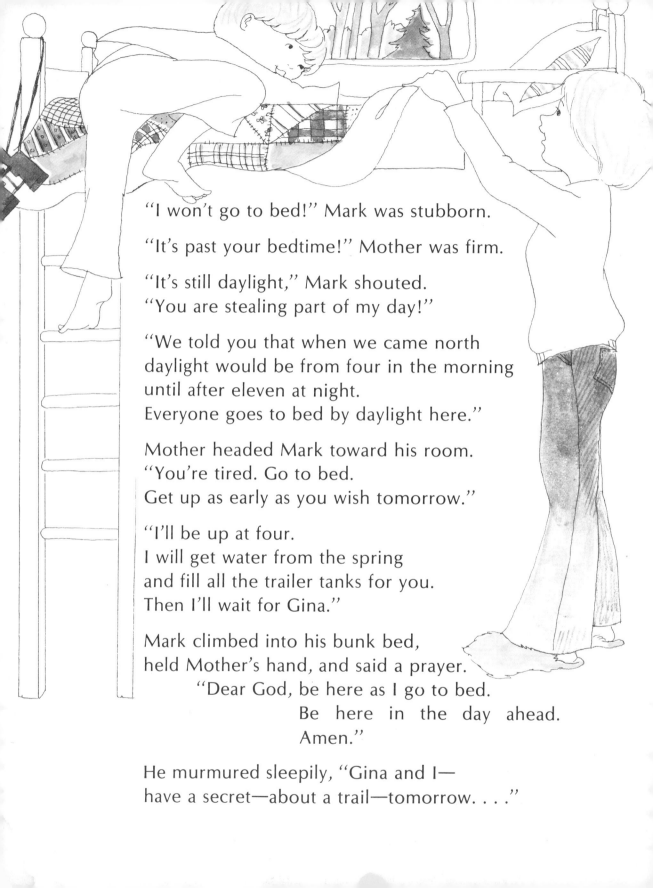

"I won't go to bed!" Mark was stubborn.

"It's past your bedtime!" Mother was firm.

"It's still daylight," Mark shouted.
"You are stealing part of my day!"

"We told you that when we came north
daylight would be from four in the morning
until after eleven at night.
Everyone goes to bed by daylight here."

Mother headed Mark toward his room.
"You're tired. Go to bed.
Get up as early as you wish tomorrow."

"I'll be up at four.
I will get water from the spring
and fill all the trailer tanks for you.
Then I'll wait for Gina."

Mark climbed into his bunk bed,
held Mother's hand, and said a prayer.
        "Dear God, be here as I go to bed.
                Be here in the day ahead.
                Amen."

He murmured sleepily, "Gina and I—
have a secret—about a trail—tomorrow. . . ."

"Are we lost?" Mark asked Gina.
He stumbled along the faint, overgrown trail.
He was scared by the dark forest.

"Lost? Course not! I've been on this trail."

"Alone?"

"No—o—o. With Daddy and with Tabera."

"Mother doesn't know where I am.
I told her we had a secret for today."

Gina was growing scared, too.
"This trail isn't the one I wanted.
I took a wrong turn," she admitted.

"You sure did! What do we do now?"

"First, we don't panic," Gina said firmly.
"Daddy says that's rule one when lost.
Second, we don't move about too much.
Tabera says that's rule two when lost."

"And then we shout," Mark said.
"Daddy says shout when lost. Rule three."

"Let's camp here and wait," Gina said.

There was a crash in the forest.

"A bear!" Mark said and moved toward Gina.

"Only a deer, or maybe a tree falling."

A scream tore through the treetops.

"An eagle!" Mark shouted.

"Probably a crow trying to scare us."

"What if no one looks for us?" Mark said.

"Your mother is probably looking already."

"What if we are here all night?" Mark asked.

"We'll build a lean-to with branches.
We'll gather leaves and boughs for a bed."

"We'll be hungry and thirsty," Mark said.

"Don't you know people can live for days
without food and water?" Gina comforted him.
"They are looking for us by now.
Let's start to shout."

"Suppose no one finds us?" Mark shivered.

"They'll bring Tabera. She reads trail signs."

They began to shout.
At last they heard answering shouts.
Mark ran into the forest. "Here! Here!" he called.

"Come back!" Gina ordered.
"That's the worst thing to do.
If we move, it is harder to find us."

Mark and Gina both shouted.
The answering shouts came nearer.
Finally three people came along the old trail.

"Mother! Daddy!" Mark screamed.

"Tabera! Tabera!" Gina screamed.

"Tabera led us," Mother said, hugging Mark.
"She came to visit you. We could not find you."

Tabera scolded Gina, "You took the old trail."

"I didn't mean to," Gina said.

"This is an old, faint trail," Tabera said.
"A shortcut. My father used it.
Shortcuts are not for children.
Better you stay on the good trails."

"Yes. And better you obey your parents.
We've told you not to go alone in the forest,"
Mark's father spoke sternly. Then he smiled.
"We're glad you are safe," he said.

They went home single file on the faint trail.

Mark looked back at Gina and grinned.
"I wasn't scared. Were you?"

Gina grinned, too, "Of course not!"

"Tomorrow is a special Sunday," Gina said.
"We will go to church."

"I go to church every Sunday at home."

"I know. In cities there are many churches.
Here there is no church.
Most Sundays Mother and Daddy and I
have our own church—just three people.
But tomorrow we will have a minister.
Everyone will come. And. . . ."

"And what?" Mark asked.

"Church will be on the lake at our house!"

On Sunday Mark put on his bright life jacket
They were going to church in the canoe.
Daddy and Mother paddled the canoe.

As they rounded the point,
Mark heard voices first, then saw the boats.

The minister came out from shore on a raft.
"Look," Mark whispered to Mother,
"he has an altar and a piano."

"It's a portable organ. Gina's mother
will play."

Gina floated up to them in her little shell boat.
"May I sit in your pew?" she whispered.

She floated close. "Tabera's here.
She always comes when there is church.
She went to mission school long ago."

Music and song floated over trees and water.
The minister said a prayer,
read from the Bible, and talked to the people.

Mark listened to the minister.
He looked at the sky, trees, water, sand.
He whispered to Father, "God is here."

When church was over, everyone landed on shore.
They talked, laughed, visited—
campers, hikers, loggers, oilmen, miners,
hunters, surveyors, engineers, Indians.
Most of them had brought lunch to eat on the shore.

Tabera's canoe floated past Mark and Gina.
"Hello, little friends.
Come soon to see me," she called.

"We will!" Gina and Mark shouted and waved.

A few days later Gina, Mark, and their mothers
were spending the day exploring by boat, landing
where they pleased.

They saw a cabin,
abandoned, tipping, sinking into the brush.

"Who lived there?" Mark's mother asked.

"It was a home built by Icelandic people
a hundred years ago," Gina's mother said.
"There were many farms along the lake.
But settlers left. Life was too hard here."

She headed the boat to shore.
Mark and Gina hopped out to beach the boat.

"How do you know about the cabin?" Mark asked.

"Because I am of Icelandic ancestry," Gina's mother
        answered.

Victoria Island

MANITOBA

ONTARIO

JAMES
BAY

"So am I!" Gina said proudly.

"My grandparents came from Iceland.
They settled at the south end of the lake
where the climate and land are not as harsh.
My family still farms there," Gina's mother
     explained.

"We visited an Icelandic town," Gina said.
"We saw a museum, historic houses, old fishing
     boats. . . ."

Gina's mother opened the cabin door.
"We also visited an Icelandic settlement
that is being preserved as an historic park."

Mark and Gina poked about in the cabin.
"Look what I found!" Mark held up a tin mug.
"Did an Icelander leave this behind?"

Gina's mother smiled. "Perhaps.
Or perhaps a careless camper left it."

That evening Mark showed Father the mug
and told him about the Icelandic settlers.

They spread the big atlas on the table.
Father chalked a wiggly line
from Iceland to their trailer on the lake.

"They were brave people to come so far," Father
     said.

"Did the forest scare them?" Mark wondered.

It was Mark's last day in the north woods.

Early in the afternoon the tow truck
would come over the rutted logging road
to pick up the trailer, Mother, Father, and Mark.

Mark was happy because he was going home.

But Mark was also sad because he was leaving
the forest, lakes, streams, beaches,
and their snug trailer home under the trees.

"Why can't I live with Gina this winter?" he asked.

Mother smiled. "You start school soon.
And Gina starts school, too."

"School! There's no school here!"

"Gina's parents get her lessons by mail.
They teach Gina at home."

Mark heard Gina call.
"Hi!" he shouted. "We're leaving today."

"I know, silly! Would I forget?
Here's a present — to open on the truck.
I'll let your mother keep it for you."

Mark's father called him to the trailer.
"Mark, do you want to give Gina a gift?"

"Oh, yes! But I have nothing to give her."

"What about your field glasses?
I know you love them. But so does Gina."

Mark hesitated, then raced to his room.
He put his field glasses into a bag.

He went to Gina. "I have a gift for you, too.
Don't open it till you are home. Promise!"

"I promise." Gina felt the knobby bag.
Her eyes grew huge.
"Thank you! I'm going now. Good-bye, Mark."

"Mother," Mark teased, "give me Gina's gift."

"No. You are to open it on the truck."

"Will I like it?"

"You will like it. Tabera made it."

"I know! I know!" Mark shouted.
"Gina has given me Tabera's driftwood bird!"

Mother and Mark looked at one another.
"Oh, hasn't it been a wonderful summer!"
They both spoke at once—and laughed together.